Good Night,
Mouse!

All rights reserved. For information about permission to
reproduce selections from this book, write to Permissions,
Houghton Mifflin Harcourt Publishing Company,
215 Park Avenue South, New York, New York 10003.

Houghton Mifflin Books for Children is an imprint of
Houghton Mifflin Harcourt Publishing Company.

www.hmhbooks.com

The text of this book is set in Arlt Blanca.
The illustrations were created with watercolors, pastels,
and colored pencils, and finished digitally.

Library of Congress Cataloging-in-Publication Data
Henry, Jed.
  Good night, Mouse! / written and illustrated by Jed Henry.
      p. cm.
  Summary: All of Mouse's friends have ideas for helping him
fall asleep.
  ISBN 978-0-547-98156-7
  [1. Sleep—Fiction. 2. Bedtime—Fiction.
3. Friendship—Fiction. 4. Mice—Fiction.
5. Animals—Fiction.] I. Title.
  PZ7.H39374Goo 2013
  [E]—dc23
2012041890

Manufactured in China
SCP 10 9 8 7 6 5 4 3 2 1
4500418591

For Tanei

Good Night,

HOUGHTON MIFFLIN BOOKS FOR CHILDREN

Mouse!

written and illustrated by

Jed Henry

Houghton Mifflin Harcourt • Boston New York 2013

How are we going to help Mouse sleep?

I know how to wear him out.

Tripping, skipping, tired tumbling.
Good night, Mouse!

Looks like Mouse is all wound up.
A bath will soothe his weary bones.

Dip and soak, dream and drift.
Good night, Mouse!

Mouse is sure to catch a chill.
I'll tuck him in a toasty bed.

Curl and snuggle, cozy cuddle.
Good night, Mouse!

No one wants a pointy pillow.
Mouse needs somewhere soft to lie.

Lazy dazing, lulling, lounging.
Good night, Mouse!

All this fluff is getting stuffy.
Fresh air puts a mouse at ease.

Glitter gleaming, sweetly dreaming,
Good night, Mouse!

Mouse's eyes are bleary blinking.
Softer light will calm his mind.

Dusky shadow, deep and dim.
Good night, Mouse!

I hear growling in the dark.
A hungry tummy haunts our friend.

Licking, smacking, midnight snacking.
Good night, Mouse!

All this frenzy frazzles Mouse.
Peace and quiet is what he needs.

Hushed and still, soft and silent.
Good night, Mouse.

Why is Mouse still awake?

Close your eyes, little Mouse—
tree frogs singing,
crickets ringing,
under moonlight's silver beam.

Rest your head, little Mouse—
stars above you,
friends who love you
stay beside you while you dream.

Good night, Mouse.